ROS

JUDY VARGA
ONCE-A-YEAR WITCH

73- 111046

William Morrow and Company   New York 1973

Varga, Judy.
  Once-a-year witch.

  SUMMARY: Booboolina's peculiar compromise in practicing
her witchcraft gives the town a unique holiday.
  [1. Witches—Fiction. 2. Halloween—Stories]
I. Title.
PZ7.V43On   [E]   72-4002
ISBN 0-688-20060-5
ISBN 0-688-30060-X (lib. bdg.)

In a ramshackle cottage above a small English town
lived Booboolina, the witch.
Her magic was strong, her spells gruesome.
Of all the witches in the country,
Booboolina was known to be the most wicked.

The townspeople were careful
not to anger Booboolina,
for she had a very bad temper.
They trembled with fear
whenever the witch appeared in the sky overhead.
Usually, however, she merely hovered at a safe distance
and watched them.
Then, one terrible Friday,
Booboolina circled the town three times
and landed right in the middle of the park.

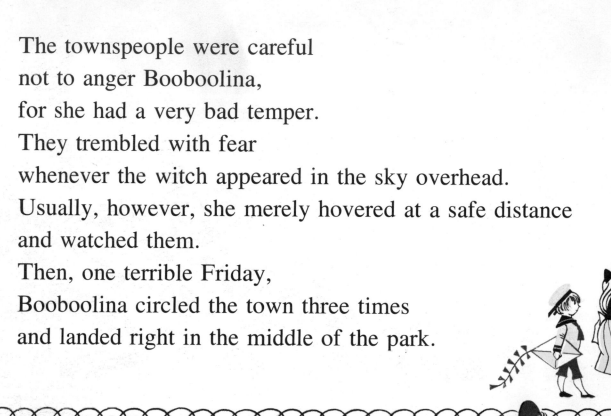

"I want one of your children," cackled Booboolina,
pointing a knobby finger at a little girl.
"You better give her to me," she shrieked,
"or I'll do some monstrous mischief."
To make her point, she raised her arms
and muttered some mumbo jumbo.
At once small whirlwinds began to dance.
They knocked people about
and carried their hats high into the sky.

Before the townspeople could say a word,
Booboolina snatched up the chosen child.
The parents tried to grab the broomstick,
but Booboolina was already out of reach.
"Please, let her go!" they pleaded.
"What do you want with her anyhow?"
"Why, I'll put her in the soup pot, of course!"
said Booboolina with a snicker,
as she soared still higher.
"And don't try to rescue her, or I'll cast a spell
that will turn all the boys into mice!"
The townspeople were shocked into silence,
and Booboolina laughed so hard
that she almost tumbled off the broomstick.
In fact, her cackles could be heard
long after she was out of sight.

The people tried to go about their business.
They hoped they never would see Booboolina again.
But on the following Friday she was back.
Balancing on her broom, she waved to the sky.
Egg-sized hailstones pelted the people
and bumped them on the head.
Nearby trees shriveled with frost;
flowers withered.

Booboolina waved her hand, and the hailstones stopped.
"I am in no mood to argue," she cackled.
"Today I want that one," she said,
pointing at another girl.

The people lived in fear of Fridays,
for each time that day of the week arrived
the witch returned without fail.
She no longered bothered to show her powers.
Casually she snatched up a girl
without even coming to a full stop.

She snatched them through windows
or pulled them out their front doors.
She found them no matter where they were hidden.
She snatched thin ones, fat ones,
pretty ones and homely ones.
"If Booboolina doesn't stop,
there'll be nary a girl left in town,"
said the people.

The men of the town held a conference.
"Somehow we must do away with the witch," they said.
At last they decided to raid the witch's lair
and take her by surprise.
The men hoped she could be done away with
before she had time
to cast a terrible spell.

They creeped and crawled up the rocky hill,
fighting off droves of angry bats.
They moved slowly, stealthily,
hoping that Booboolina would not hear them come.

At close hand Booboolina's cottage
looked even worse than it did from afar.
Gingerly the men shoved open a creaky door.
"What have we here?"
they said, and recoiled in horror.
The parlor was a disgusting place even for a witch.
Big black ravens picked at small white bones
scattered over the dusty floor.
Fat spiders and hairy bats hung among the cobwebs,
warty toads lolled everywhere.
Musty jars with hideous contents
lined one entire wall.
And there, in an alcove, stood the witch's cauldron,
bubbling evilly.
"Oh, our poor children!" the men said, sighing.

Booboolina's hat and cape
hung on a hook on the wall,
but there was no sign of the witch herself.
All was quiet, all was still.
Then suddenly, from way in the back,
they heard Booboolina's cackling laughter.
The men hurried through a cluttered storeroom,
stumbling over wicked-eyed witch cats,
upsetting frothing crocks of mischief potions.
They tore away the dusty black curtains,
which blocked their way,
and stood in the narrow opening not believing their eyes.

The Cauldron

Traveling Cauldron

Spell No. 1

mbay, chava
ava kava
kava kava
wa chava

The Hat

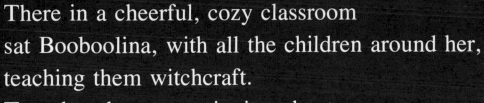

There in a cheerful, cozy classroom
sat Booboolina, with all the children around her,
teaching them witchcraft.
Together they were singing chants
and practising spells.
Every so often Booboolina gave them an adoring smile.
She loved little girls,
for they were what future witches were made of.

The men burst into the room
and tied a kerchief around Booboolina's mouth,
before she had a chance to utter a single spell.
"Run children," they shouted.
"We will hold the witch here
until you are safely away."

But the children gathered around Booboolina.
"We'd rather stay!" they said.
"We like her,
and it's fun being a witch."

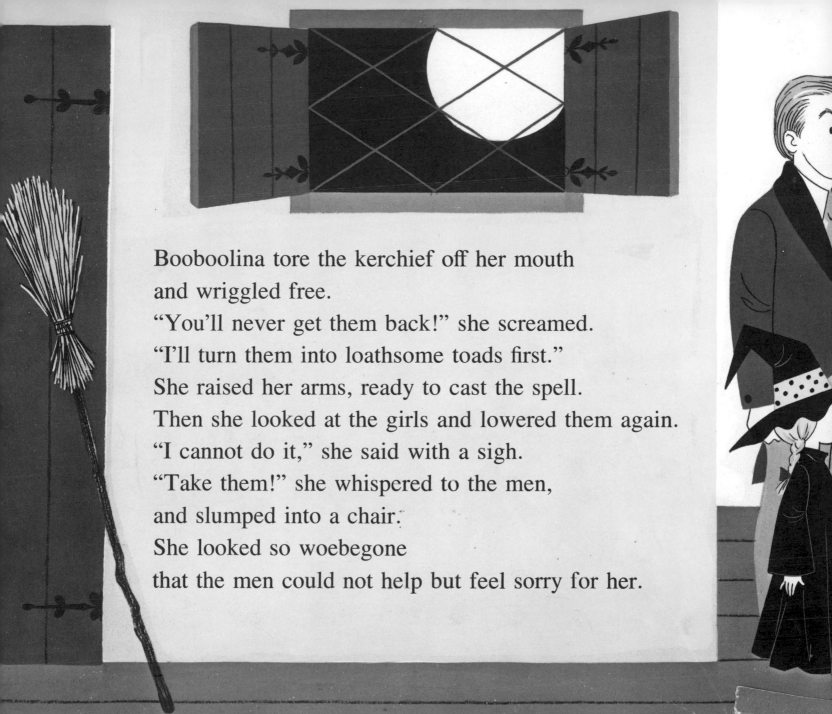

Booboolina tore the kerchief off her mouth
and wriggled free.
"You'll never get them back!" she screamed.
"I'll turn them into loathsome toads first."
She raised her arms, ready to cast the spell.
Then she looked at the girls and lowered them again.
"I cannot do it," she said with a sigh.
"Take them!" she whispered to the men,
and slumped into a chair.
She looked so woebegone
that the men could not help but feel sorry for her.

"You may come and visit the children
whenever you like, you silly witch," said the men.
But Booboolina only wailed louder.
"I cannot!" she bawled.
"A witch cannot just pop in for tea!
I have my reputation in witchdom to worry about."
The men put their heads together.
"You could visit them once a year," they said.
"The girls can dress like witches for that one night,
and no one will notice you at all.
Watch for lantern lights in the houses.
They will signal that we're ready for you."
Booboolina stopped wailing and nodded her head.
She was so pleased that she flew them all home
on her extra-long broomstick.

"Just one more thing," said the men as they parted,
"no more child snatching,
or we'll tell all witchdom how soft-hearted you are."

And so, on a dark October night
when jack-o-lanterns flickered in every home,
Booboolina flew into town.
All the children, dressed in eerie outfits,
were there to welcome her.
If there were other witches watching
among all the bats, ghosts, and goblins
they never would have noticed
Booboolina among her once-a-year witches.
Booboolina wasted no time.
"And now we'll proceed
with your education," she cackled,
as she rushed the girls off to a quiet spot.

When the lesson was over,
the girls called at every door.
"Would you like to see our new tricks?" they asked.
"Oh dear!" people said.
"Wouldn't you rather have some candy instead?"
Anxious to please, they gave Booboolina and the girls
treats of goodies to take home.
After all, even once-a-year witches
might cause some mischief with their magic spells.
As the moon sank low
and Booboolina mounted her broom,
preparing for takeoff, everyone shouted,
"Have a safe trip!
See you next year."

To this day, children everywhere
stay up late on the last night of October,
knocking on doors, crying "Trick or Treat!"
They are celebrating Halloween, the night of the year
when goblins dance, witches ride,
and ghosts howl with the wind.